returned w/

2/07

KLOOZ

Detective's Duel

by J. Banscherus

translated by Daniel C. Baron

illustrated by Ralf Butschkow

Librarian Reviewer
Marci Peschke
Librarian, Dallas Independent School District
MA Education Reading Specialist, Stephen F. Austin State University
Learning Resources Endorsement, Texas Women's University

Reading Consultant
Mary Evenson
Middle School Teacher, Edina Public Schools, MN
MA in Education, University of Minnesota

STONE ARCH BOOKS
Minneapolis   San Diego

First published in the United States in 2007
by Stone Arch Books,
151 Good Counsel Drive, P.O. Box 669,
Mankato, Minnesota 56002
www.stonearchbooks.com

First published by Arena Books,
Rottendorfer str. 16, D-97074,
Würzburg, Germany

Copyright © 1999 Jürgen Banscherus
Illustrations copyright © 1999 Ralf Butschkow

Library of Congress Cataloging-in-Publication Data
Banscherus, Jürgen.
  [Duell der Detektive. English]
  Detective's Duel / by J. Banscherus; translated by Daniel C. Baron;
illustrated by Ralf Butschkow.
  p. cm. — (Pathway Books – Klooz)
  Summary: When a new boy comes to town and starts taking cases
away from Klooz, they decide to have a duel to find the best detective
in town.
  ISBN-13: 978-1-59889-339-7 (library binding)
  ISBN-10: 1-59889-339-4 (library binding)
  ISBN-13: 978-1-59889-434-9 (paperback)
  ISBN-10: 1-59889-434-X (paperback)
  [1. Detectives—Fiction. 2. Friendship—Fiction. 3. Mystery and
detective stories.] I. Baron, Daniel C. II. Butschkow, Ralf, ill. III. Title.
PZ7.B22927De 2007
[Fic]—dc22   2006027191

Art Director: Heather Kindseth
Graphic Designer: Kay Fraser

1 2 3 4 5 6 12 11 10 09 08 07

TOP SECRET

Table of contents

Chapter **1** A Kid Called King 5

Chapter **2** The Duel 17

Chapter **3** Olga is Suspicious 30

Chapter **4** Setting a Trap 41

Chapter **5** The Silver Star 48

KLOOZ
Detective's
Duel

CHAPTER 1

A Kid Called King

During spring break I flew with my mom to Mexico. It was really nice there. The sea and sky were sparkling blue. The beach was full of sand. So was our hotel room. But for a private detective like me, there just wasn't much to do.

Once I found an expensive pair of sunglasses that someone from our hotel had lost. Another time I stopped an air mattress slasher from doing his dirty work.

That criminal thought that what he was doing was funny. Weird! Other than that, there wasn't much going on.

Two weeks of sun, sand, and sea. It almost got on my nerves.

That's why I was happy to finally be able to fly back home.

Nothing exciting happened until a few weeks after I returned.

After a short time I realized that no one needed a private detective. There were stories in the newspaper about robberies and con artists, but I didn't get even the smallest case.

I got so desperate that I would have taken the case of a missing dog! And that is the last thing that a real private detective wants.

But I didn't even get a missing mouse case. The telephone never rang and no one except for the mail carrier or a salesperson ever rang our doorbell.

During this time I chewed gum like crazy. My favorite Carpenter's chewing gum was with me from morning until night.

It helped me pass the terrible hours of the day.

Soon my Carpenter's supply was nearly gone. I had to go to Olga's newspaper stand to buy some more.

"I haven't seen you in a while," Olga greeted me. "How is it going?"

"It's going," I said. "Give me five packs of Carpenter's."

She pushed five packs across the counter.

"What's wrong, Klooz?" she asked.

"Nothing's wrong," I grumbled.

Olga stared at me. She didn't believe me.

"No one needs a good private detective," I explained. "That's what's wrong."

Olga patted me on the cheek.

"That happens," she said. "My business has seen better days too."

I quickly took a step back. When Olga pats me on the cheek, the next thing she wants to do is hug me.

Hugging I can live without, even from one of my oldest friends. And I mean "oldest" in a good way.

"I have a feeling that you'll have a new case tomorrow," she said.

"We'll see," I said. I started to go.

Olga held me back.

"There is something I have to tell you," she whispered, even though there wasn't a soul around. "You have a twin."

"Me? A twin?" I said.

Olga explained that while I was away in Mexico, she had a new customer.

He was a little older than me, chewed Carpenter's nonstop like me, and wore a vest like me. And he had a baseball cap with a K on it, just like I did!

"Probably a fan," I said.

Olga chuckled. "Could be," she said, "but I heard him talking to another boy about a case."

"What kind of a case?" I asked. A detective case? Hmm, was this kid moving in on my territory?

Olga shrugged.

"I'm not sure what kind of case, Klooz," she said. "You know it isn't very nice to listen in on other people's conversations."

"Yeah, right!" I said.

Olga just smiled.

Olga is as curious as I am about other people. She finds out every little thing that happens in her part of the neighborhood.

"Do you know the name of this kid?" I asked.

"He said to call him King," Olga said.

Olga laughed.

"King? That isn't a name for a boy!" she said.

King was a cool name.

Was it cooler than Klooz? I wondered.

As I walked home, I thought about what Olga told me.

There was a strange kid out there who was imitating me and talking about a case.

What if this boy was working as a private detective?

What if he was taking work away from me?

What if everyone was asking him for help instead of asking me?

That would explain why I wasn't getting any new cases.

The guy moved in while I was on vacation and took over my stomping grounds!

I was only gone for two weeks and he steals all my work.

Just you wait, King. You don't know Klooz.

Nobody gets rid of me that easily.

As soon as I got home, I grabbed the phone and called everyone I knew.

I needed to find out more about this King. No one I talked to had heard of King until I called Robert, a kid from my class.

"Yes, there's a guy who wears a cap like that at my youth center," he said. "In fact, his cap looks just like the one you always wear."

"With a K, right?" I said.

"Yeah, a big K," said Robert.

"He calls himself King," said Robert, "but his name is really Herman."

Herman?

If my name were Herman, I'd probably call myself King too.

"Is he at the youth center every afternoon?" I asked.

Robert thought for a moment.

"No, not every afternoon. Just once in a while," he replied.

I left my homework for later and grabbed my ballcap. It was the cap with the K on it. I was the first one in town to wear a cap like this, and no one was going to change that!

I decided to go make a little stop at the youth center.

Perhaps I would be lucky and find this guy King, the guy who was stealing my cases.

"Where are you going?" my mother asked.

"To catch a thief," I said.

CHAPTER 2

The Duel

There wasn't much going on at the youth center. A few girls were listening to their iPods, others were playing video games, and a few boys were playing pool.

One guy was trying to sink a ball in the corner pocket. He was wearing a vest and a baseball cap with a big K on it. He was also chewing gum. It had to be Carpenter's.

Pool didn't seem to be his game. The
guy shot the ball and missed the hole by
at least a foot. After the shot I went up
to him. "Hey, Herman," I said.

He made a face at the mention of "Herman." Then he got himself under control. "The name is King," he said.

"I know, Herman," I said.

The boy spit his gum into the trash can in the corner. He had good aim. "What do you want, Klooz?" he asked.

"You know me?" I was shocked.

"Of course," he answered. "You used to work as a detective, right?"

Used to? I wanted to strangle the guy, but I hate violence.

I said, "You've got no business in my part of town, Herman. This is my beat. Take your detective business somewhere else."

"Why should I?" he asked.

"Because this is my territory," I said. "It always has been. By the way, I think it's really dumb that you're trying to copy everything I do."

King laughed. "First of all, this is a free country," he said. "Second, I can wear whatever I want to wear. People call me King. That's why I have the K on my cap. Wearing a vest keeps me warm. And Carpenter's chewing gum is the best. Any other questions?"

I didn't reply.

He put his hands in his pockets and said, "You should probably just give it up, Klooz. There isn't enough room for two detectives in this part of town."

I was speechless.

I had solved the most difficult cases and survived the most dangerous situations. Now this guy comes along and thinks he's better than I am?

"You're right," I said. "There's only room for one detective in this town: the best detective. So let's just find out who the best detective is."

King thought about this.

"How about a duel?" I said. "Whoever loses doesn't work as a detective anymore — at least not in this part of town."

King cracked a crooked smile. "It's a deal," he said. "So how do we work this duel?"

I grabbed a newspaper. Together we looked through it for the right case.

"There!" I said, pointing at a headline. It said: "More Dead Fish In The Noon Street Swimming Pool."

The article said, "Dead fish have been found in a local outdoor swimming pool. Police and city officials are puzzled. The pool had to be closed to swimmers until the water could be cleaned."

"That's it!" I said.

King nodded. "Doesn't really matter which case you pick. You're going to lose, Klooz."

"We'll see about that, Hermy."

King grinned and then took off. I left too. If I wanted to win this duel, I had no time to lose.

I had to stake out the swimming pool and wait for the crooks to return to the scene of the crime.

If the evil fish throwers didn't show up tonight, I would have to keep coming back until they did. I had to win the duel!

My mom had a book club to go to with her friends. She left the house right before nine o'clock.

That's when I headed out too. I packed two bottles of milk, a warm sweatshirt, and a flashlight in my backpack.

I also put a pack of Carpenter's gum in my pocket.

When I got to the Noon Street Park, it was getting dark. After a short search I found a hole in the chain link fence.

I crawled through it. I had been there before, to swim, of course. Now it looked empty and spooky.

The moon cast a ghostly shine on the water.

I wondered if King was around. Maybe I was lucky and his parents didn't let him go out at night.

I made myself comfortable behind a bush.

From there I could see the whole area: the pool itself, the park building, and the entrance and exit.

If someone threw any dead fish into the pool, I would see them.

It was cold that night. I put on my sweatshirt. Still, my teeth chattered so loud that I sounded like a woodpecker. Then I fell asleep.

I was rudely awakened by someone shaking me.

"What's going on?" I said without even opening my eyes.

"Wake up!" said an unfriendly voice. "And make it snappy!"

I opened my eyes. Standing in front of me was the head lifeguard. I knew him from last summer.

"What are you doing here?" he asked. "Did you run away from home?"

I shook my head.

"How did you get in here?" he demanded.

I shrugged my shoulders.

"You better start talking," he said as I stood up.

I could see it was starting to get light. Morning was coming.

"Otherwise I'm calling the police," he said. "They can pick you up and bring you home."

"Okay," I said. I sighed.

I explained that I was on a stakeout for the people who were throwing the dead fish into the pool.

The lifeguard laughed.

"What's so funny?" I asked.

"There must be a detective factory around here somewhere," he said. "There was already another one here last night."

Suddenly I got a really bad feeling.

"And?" I asked.

"He was a guy about your age," the lifeguard explained. "He caught the fish throwers. It was a good thing he had a cell phone with him. He called us right away and the police arrested them. What a great kid. As a reward we've given him a free pool pass."

"Ah," I mumbled. I couldn't think of anything else to say.

"Don't you want to know who the fish throwers were?" the guard asked.

"Um, sure," I said.

"It was a couple of boys who liked to fish. They thought they were being funny. Funny!" he complained.

"Yeah, funny," I whispered.

The lifeguard let me out through the main entrance.

He called to me as I left, but I didn't hear what he said.

Nothing really mattered to me now. I had lost the duel with King.

From now on, this part of town belonged to him.

As I was crawling through the fence earlier, he was probably already in bed. If only I had started two hours earlier, I could have caught the fish throwers myself. Man, was I stupid!

CHAPTER 3

Olga Is Suspicious

I got home just in time. I had just thrown my backpack into my room and turned on the coffeemaker for my mom when she walked into the kitchen. Boy, was that close.

Luckily my mom had gone right to sleep after the book club. Otherwise I would have been in deep trouble that morning, and I didn't need any more trouble.

My mom gave me a kiss. "You're a little late," she said, and placed fresh donuts on the kitchen table.

"I overslept," I said.

"Do you feel okay?" she asked. "Are you sick?"

I shook my head. I felt a lump in my throat that was getting bigger and bigger. I felt like if I opened my mouth I would start crying. That was something that I really didn't want.

After my mom poured her coffee, she gave me a big hug.

"Have something to eat," she said. "Then you'll feel better."

If she only knew, I thought. If she only knew.

* * *

I don't know how I survived the school day. I must have looked pretty scary, because both my teachers and classmates left me alone.

Even during recess no one spoke to me. I probably didn't have a real friendly look on my face. I had been beaten by King and I just couldn't accept that.

After school I just had one thought. I wanted to go home and go to bed. The night at the swimming pool had worn me out.

King was waiting for me at the entrance of school.

"Well?" he said with a grin.

"Congratulations," I snarled as I tried to get by him.

He grabbed me by the vest and asked, "Don't you want to know how I caught those bad guys?"

I shook my head. "No interest, you won fair and square."

King laughed. "Don't take it so hard, Klooz. Sooner or later, everyone meets someone better than they are."

"You aren't better than me, Herman," I growled. I was just dumb, I said to myself.

King wouldn't let me walk past him.

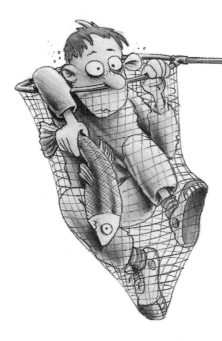

He kept bragging about his case. "I suspected that the fish throwers let themselves be locked in the pool as it closed," he explained. "After all, who goes to a swimming pool in the middle of the night in order to throw dead fish in the water? So, after it closed I showed up, and bang! I caught them. I used my cell phone and three minutes later the lifeguard took care of the rest. The fish throwers probably felt pretty stupid."

"I'll bet," I said.

"Not bad detective work, huh?" King said as he pulled a cell phone out of his vest. "This is exactly what a detective needs nowadays."

I didn't say another word. I just went home.

One more word from that arrogant King and I might have forgotten my good manners.

On the other hand, King was clever. I had thought that the fish throwers would wait until dark to start their dirty work, but I was completely wrong.

When I showed up at the swimming pool, the whole case was already finished. A cell phone probably was a good piece of detective equipment.

Of course I didn't need to think about that now.

I wasn't supposed to work as a detective anymore, so I could just forget about getting a cell phone.

I needed a sympathetic listener, so I went to visit Olga.

"Just look at you!" she said. "Are you sick?"

That's just what my mother had said. I must have looked as sick as a dog.

"No I'm not sick," I replied. "Please give me a glass of Coke, Olga."

"Coke? You never drink Coke," she said.

"Today I need one," I said. Then I told her everything that had happened.

"King is a better detective," I said as I ended my story. "Now this neighborhood belongs to him."

"No!" she said.

"Yes!" I replied.

"That's a load of garbage," she muttered as she slid the cola across the counter. "You're still the best detective I know, Klooz."

"I lost the duel," I said. "I can't work anymore."

Olga stuck a piece of candy in her mouth. "And what if this King had tricked you somehow?" she said.

That got my attention. "What do you mean?" I asked.

"Well, it could be that he had inside information. Maybe he knew when the guys were going to throw the fish."

I shook my head. "I picked the case from the newspaper. We could have just as easily picked a different case."

"So what?" Olga replied. "What does that prove? He still could have worked with the fish throwers, Klooz. It's like a firefighter who lights a house on fire just so he can put out the fire a few minutes later."

Holy cow! Olga could be right!

King solved the case quickly—
too quickly.

And he was too sure of himself.

"Thanks, Olga," I cried. "Without you I would have given up. But now King will get what's coming to him. I promise you that!"

Olga smiled. "I always have faith in you, kid."

"King is a customer of yours," I said.
"Maybe you could find out which case he's working on next. Then I could follow him around and find out how he works."

"I'll do anything for you, Klooz," Olga said.

CHAPTER 4

Setting a Trap

In the next few days I talked with lots of people and asked lots of questions.

It was always the same.

Everyone who had worked with King had great things to say about him.

He solved his cases quickly, sometimes after just a few hours. As his fee he asked for only three packs of Carpenter's gum.

That was two fewer packs than me!

There wasn't anyone who thought King might be up to no good. He seemed as clean as a freshly washed baby.

A week later, I went back to visit Olga to buy some more Carpenter's chewing gum. She seemed to be waiting for me.

"My star!" she called out. "My star!"

Usually she called me "sweetie."

Even "my dear" would have been okay. But "my star" just sounded dumb.

"I don't mean you, Klooz," she said. "Some criminals stole the metal star from my car's hood last night."

Olga had bought a wonderful old car the week before. It was a dream come true for her.

She parked it across the street from her newspaper stand and never let it out of her sight.

"Do you have any idea who could have done it?" I asked.

Olga shook her head. "The car looks horrible now!" she said. She pointed to the space where her car was parked.

"It still looks great," I said. "Did you go to the police yet?"

"Because of a stolen star?" she asked. "They have better things to do with their time."

I guess she was right.

At that moment I had a brilliant idea, and the more I thought about it, the more I thought it was the idea of the century.

SHERLOCK HOLMES

Even Sherlock Holmes would have been jealous.

"Could you get the star replaced?" I asked.

"Of course," she answered, "but I am not sure I should. What happens if they just steal it again?"

"That's the idea," I explained.

Olga looked at me as if I had told her to eat pickled worms.

"Are you crazy?" she asked.

"Crazy like a fox," I said. "When was the last time King was here?"

"Hmm, a week ago."

"Then he must be running out of Carpenter's," I said.

"Could be," Olga replied. "But what does that have to do with my star?"

"A lot," I answered.

"You're a hopeless case, Klooz," Olga said.

I laughed. "Together we will set a trap for my buddy King. Will you help me, Olga?"

"For you, Klooz? Anything!"

I explained my whole plan to Olga before her next customer came.

She was so excited that she gave me a free can of pop and a pack of Carpenter's.

I strolled home. If our plan worked, King would be finished and I would be back in the detective business!

"You look happy," my mother said when I arrived home.

"I am," I answered.

She looked at me thoughtfully. "A new case?" she asked.

"A new case?" I repeated, and thought for a moment. Not really.

This was even bigger! This was a duel of detectives.

"Let's eat," said my mom. "Then you can tell me all about it."

CHAPTER 5

The Silver Star

The next day after lunch, I ran to Olga's newsstand.

I was dying to find out if King had showed up for his gum.

A couple of construction workers were there. They were buying everything Olga had. I had to wait for what seemed like forever before she had time for me.

"King took the bait," she whispered to me excitedly.

"What did you tell him?" I asked.

Olga grinned. "I told him I was afraid for my beautiful star," she answered as she pointed to her car. A new silver star gleamed in the sunlight. "That's what we agreed I should tell him, Klooz. Right?"

"Right," I said. "And what else?"

"He asked where I lived and where I parked the car at night."

Olga slid a can of cola across the counter to me. "It's on the house, Klooz. So how did I do?"

"Perfect," I said. "You'd make a great actress."

"I like detective work," Olga purred.

"Nothing can go wrong now," I said.

I stayed at home all afternoon. I was more excited than I had ever been.

I kept going back and forth between my bedroom and the refrigerator in the kitchen.

I don't know how much yogurt I must have eaten. I couldn't think about doing my homework.

Even my favorite Carpenter's didn't calm me down. For the first time since I had discovered the gum at Olga's, it tasted like a rubber tire.

I usually drank milk by the gallon, but I wasn't in the mood.

It would have soured before it reached my stomach.

* * *

Olga always closed her newsstand around eight o'clock. It took her fifteen minutes to drive home. I would be in my hiding spot at 8:15.

My mother had been invited to a friend's. When she visited friends, she usually stayed until late in the night. So when I left the house, it was starting to get dark.

In my backpack, my two bottles of milk clinked together.

Waiting made me thirsty. I knew that from my countless nighttime stakeouts.

When I reached the front of Olga's house, I hid behind a trash bin. I had just made myself comfortable when Olga drove up. She parked her car across the street from where I was hiding.

Then she went into her house without looking left or right. I was impressed. Not even Sherlock Holmes would have suspected that she was involved in setting up a trap.

By ten o'clock, it was getting colder. I put on my thick sweater and gloves that I had brought along just in case. Even with them on, I was still freezing. Nighttime stakeouts should really only happen in summer.

Why hadn't King shown up? Were we wrong about him? My mother might be getting home any minute. If she looked in my bed and found it empty, there would be an earthquake.

I was about to leave my stakeout when a figure came down the street. I stayed in my hiding place.

The figure I saw was definitely suspicious. He kept looking around, staying in the shadows, and trying not to make any noise. He was wearing a hood even though it wasn't raining.

I couldn't see his face.

It was Olga's star stealer! I would have bet a hundred packs of Carpenter's on it.

Carefully, I placed the bottle of milk I had just finished on the ground and got myself ready.

In a moment, King would make his move. I was already looking forward to the surprised look on his face when I jumped out of my hiding place.

In the meantime, the figure had moved closer to my hiding place.

He stood directly in front of Olga's car and then bent down as if he had to tie his shoes.

That's when everything happened, and happened quickly.

While still kneeling, the figure reached up to grab Olga's star.

I quickly raced toward him. Another figure dashed from the shadows and threw himself at the thief.

When I reached them, I grabbed someone's leg. I couldn't tell who it belonged to in the darkness.

Then I grabbed the thief's hood and tore it back to expose his face.

What?

It couldn't be true!

The figure wasn't King! It was another boy. I had never seen him before in my life.

And King?

He was lying on top of the thief, grinning at me.

"Would you please let go of my leg?" he said to me.

When we stood up, King asked the boy, "Where is the star?"

"You guys are crazy!" the boy cried. "I was just walking by here minding my own business."

"Where is the star?" King asked again.

"What star?" said the boy.

I pointed at the car. "The star you stole from Olga's car yesterday."

"You're nuts," the boy replied.

"Of course, we could go to the police," King said. "What do you think they would find if they searched your house?"

The boy sighed and pulled a silver star from his pocket.

"Here you go," he said.

I took the star from him. It felt warm.

"Now get lost," King said to the boy. "And don't let us ever catch you here again, got it?"

The boy nodded and then ran off down the street.

King punched me in the shoulder and said, "Well, Klooz, a little too late again, huh?"

I had nothing to say, and that didn't happen very often.

"You thought I stole the star, didn't you?" King said.

I just shrugged.

Could King read minds? I wondered.

"You thought I set up all of my cases myself. And tonight you wanted to trap me, you and your friend Olga, right?" King said.

Once again I just shrugged. King was getting even more unbelievable.

He stuck a piece of Carpenter's in his mouth.

"Want one, Klooz?" he asked.

"I have my own," I growled.

It's all over, I thought to myself. A guy like King comes along and makes me look like a loser.

Until he showed up, I had always been the best detective.

Now, compared to King, I felt like a beginner.

"Don't you want to know how I solve my cases so quickly?" King asked.

"Whatever," I said.

"It's my computer," he said.

He went on, "Computers are amazing. My computer showed me that there had never been a stolen star in Olga's neighborhood. By her newsstand, yes, but not here by her house. That's why I thought you were just trying to trap me."

First a cell phone and now a computer. When I listened to King talk about his detective equipment, I felt like a guy who was living in a time before there were cars.

"It's over, King," I said. "The neighborhood belongs to you."

He patted Olga's car. Then he said, "Everything is going to stay just the way it is for you, Klooz. I'm moving to another city. My mom got a new job."

"Your mom? What about your dad?" I guess that was a personal question, but it just slipped out.

"He left us a few years ago," he said.

"Mine too," I said.

We stood there for a few moments in silence.

Then King held out his hand. "I've got to go, Klooz. Too bad. We could've been a great team. You with your imagination and me with my computer."

"And your cell phone," I said.

"Exactly," he answered, and grinned. We shook hands.

Then we walked down Olga's street. At the corner, one of us went left and the other one went right. Only the car remained behind. The silver star gleamed on the hood.

* * *

That is the story of the duel of the detectives. Ever since then I have been looking at computer magazines and ads for cell phones.

My mom says we don't have the money for those kinds of things. I don't know, maybe we will someday.

What happened to King? I have no idea. The guy vanished as quickly as he had appeared. He loaded up on Carpenter's chewing gum at Olga's one more time, and that was it.

A few days after he left, Olga showed me a baseball cap with a K on it. "He gave me this," she said. "A nice boy, that Herman."

"Not Herman," I said. "He was King. If anyone was the King, he was."

The end

About the Author

Jürgen Banscherus is a worldwide phenomenon.
There are almost a million Klooz books in print,
and they have been translated into Spanish,
Danish, Thai, Chinese, and eleven other
languages. He has worked as a newspaper writer,
a research scientist, and a teacher. His first book
for children was published in 1985. He lives with
his family in Germany.

About the Illustrator

Ralf Butschkow was born in Berlin. He works as
a freelance graphic designer and illustrator, and
has published more than 50 books for children.
Critics have praised his work as "thoroughly
enjoyable," "creatively original," and "highly
recommended."

Glossary

beat (BEET)—detective talk for the area where a detective hangs out and solves crime; their town or neighborhood

duel (DOOL)—a special contest or challenge between two people

imitating (IM-uh-tay-ting)—copying, acting the same way as someone else

stakeout (STAYK-owt)—a close watch on a location, a criminal, or someone suspected of a crime

stomping grounds—(STOMP-ing growndz) a place where a person lives or likes to hang out

suspicious (suss-PISH-us)—thinking or feeling that something is wrong; or acting in a way that makes people think something is wrong

Discussion Questions

1. When Klooz first meets King, he calls him Herman. He refuses to call him King. Why does he do this?

2. Olga is Klooz's best friend. She also has a business to run. Do you think she should still sell chewing gum to King even though he won the duel against Klooz? Why or why not?

3. Why is Klooz upset when he first hears about the mysterious King?

Writing Prompts

1. Klooz and King are almost twins. The two boys dress alike, act alike, and both want to be detectives. What would you do if you met someone who acted and dressed just like you? Describe your first meeting.

2. Olga risks losing the star on her car to help Klooz set a trap. Have you ever helped out a friend even when it wasn't easy? Describe what happened.

3. What do you think would happen if King stayed in town and didn't move away at the end of the story? Would he and Klooz form their own detective agency? Or would they try to steal mystery cases from each other? Would there be another duel?

More Klooz for

After School Ghost Hunter

Klooz's school has spirit! A ghost, in fact. Mr. Boston, the janitor, claims the hallways are haunted. Klooz doesn't believe in ghosts, so he'll investigate after school. But if there aren't any ghosts, then what's that dark figure standing in the shadows?

Mystery Fans!

The Great Snake Swindle

Klooz has a lot to learn on his very first mystery case. It all starts with a kid named Snake and a handful of magic, mysterious balls. Do the balls really bring good luck to their owners? Klooz has to find the answer fast, even if it means losing his best friend.

Internet Sites

Do you want to know more about subjects related to this book? Or are you interested in learning about other topics? Then check out FactHound, a fun, easy way to find Internet sites.

Our investigative staff has already sniffed out great sites for you!

Here's how to use FactHound:

1. Visit *www.facthound.com*

2. Select your grade level.

3. To learn more about subjects related to this book, type in the book's ISBN number: **1598893394**.

4. Click the **Fetch It** button.

FactHound will fetch the best Internet sites for you!